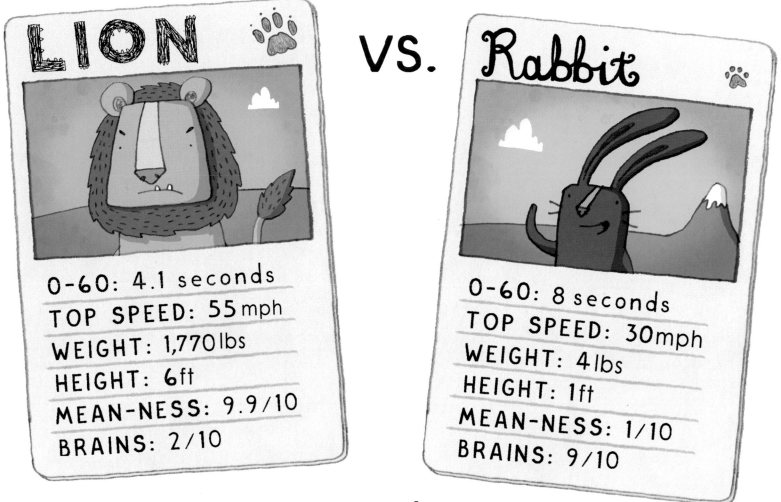

LION

0-60: 4.1 seconds
TOP SPEED: 55mph
WEIGHT: 1,770lbs
HEIGHT: 6ft
MEAN-NESS: 9.9/10
BRAINS: 2/10

VS. Rabbit

0-60: 8 seconds
TOP SPEED: 30mph
WEIGHT: 4lbs
HEIGHT: 1ft
MEAN-NESS: 1/10
BRAINS: 9/10

by Alex Latimer

PEACHTREE
ATLANTA

In memory of my mother, Margery

Published by
PEACHTREE PUBLISHERS
1700 Chattahoochee Avenue
Atlanta, Georgia 30318-2112
www.peachtree-online.com

Text and illustrations © 2013 by Alex Latimer

Originally published in Great Britain in 2013 by Picture Corgi, an imprint of Random House Children's Books.
First United States edition published in 2013 by Peachtree Publishers.

Illustrations created as pencil drawings, digitized, then finished with color and texture.

Printed in April 2013 by Toppan Leefung in China
10 9 8 7 6 5 4 3 2 1
First Edition

Library of Congress Cataloging-in-Publication Data

Latimer, Alex, author, illustrator.
Lion vs. Rabbit / by Alex Latimer.
pages cm
Summary: "Lion is mean to everyone. When the other animals can't take his bullying anymore, they hire Rabbit to outsmart him"—Provided by publisher.
ISBN-13: 978-1-56145-709-0 / ISBN-10: 1-56145-709-4
[1. Lions—Fiction. 2. Rabbits—Fiction. 3. Animals—Fiction. 4. Bullies—Fiction. 5. Contests—Fiction.] I. Title. II. Title: Lion versus Rabbit.
PZ7.L369612Li 2013
[E]—dc23
2012044982

Lion was mean to everyone.

One afternoon he gave
Buffalo a wedgie,

he stuck a silly note
on Zebra's back,

and he stole Hyena's
lunch monkey.

Soon all the animals were tired of his bullying.

LION MUST STOP NOW! (please)

They needed help, so they asked Baboon
to write an advertisement.

A bear saw the ad and arrived on the next flight.

 The bear was strong, but he was no match for Lion.

Then a moose arrived.

I'll make Lion stop!

But Lion was
too quick
for the moose.

Next came a tiger.

Lion won again.

The bear, the moose, and the tiger
all caught the next plane home.

It seemed that no one could stop Lion
from being so mean.

But just as Lion was about
to go back to his bullying,
one last animal arrived.

WAIT!

It was a rabbit.

"You're small," said Lion,
"I'll let you choose the contest."

"All right," said Rabbit. "Let's have a
marshmallow-eating competition."

"Ha!" said Lion. "That'll be easy."

Lion ate three buckets of marshmallows before he started to feel sick.

But Rabbit ate ten buckets!

"No fair," said Lion.
"I wasn't feeling well."

"Very well then," replied Rabbit.
"Let's have a quiz."

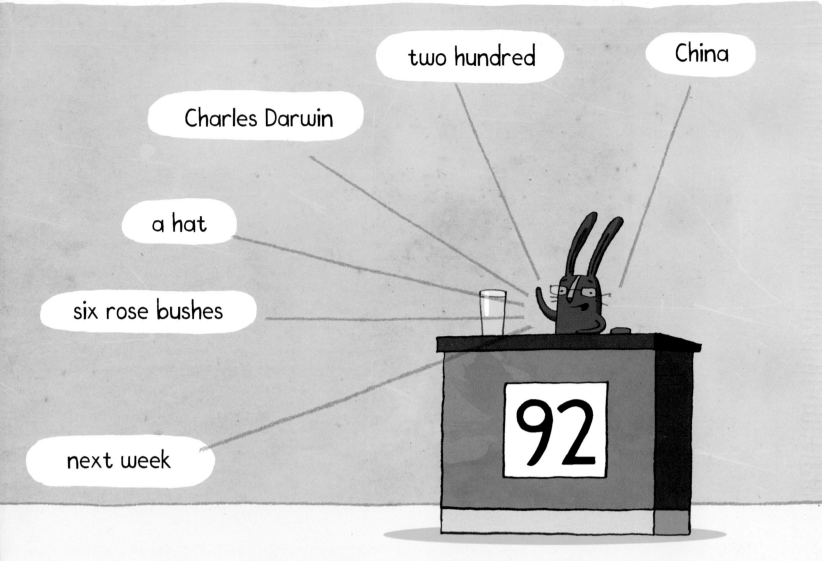

But Rabbit won the quiz easily.

"No fair!" said Lion.
"I wasn't ready."

"Okay, let's have a hopping competition," replied Rabbit.

Lion started out really well, but he only lasted ten minutes.

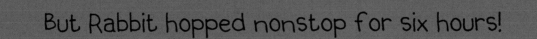

But Rabbit hopped nonstop for six hours!

"No fair," whined Lion.
"I wasn't warmed up."

"I see," replied Rabbit.
"Let's have a painting
competition."

Lion's picture was okay.

But Rabbit's picture was much better.

"No fair," moaned Lion. "I was distracted."

"All right then, we'll have one more competition," Rabbit replied. "You can choose what it is."

Lion thought hard.

"Let's race to the top of the mountain.
I'm faster and stronger
and a better climber.
There's no way I can lose!"

Lion began running before the starter pistol went off.

BANG!

START

But after a few minutes,
Lion saw Rabbit up ahead of him.

? ? ?

Lion sprinted to catch up
and overtook Rabbit.

But when he clambered up some rocks, he saw Rabbit ahead of him again.

Lion overtook Rabbit once more and raced to the top of the mountain.

But as he got close . . .

. . . he saw that Rabbit was already at the top!

"You're amazing," said Lion
(when he finally got there).
"You win. I'll stop bullying the animals."

That night, all the animals gathered at
the harbor to give Rabbit his prize and
wish him a safe journey home.

But to their surprise, there wasn't
just one rabbit leaving on the boat...

There were ten rabbits full of marshmallows,

one brainy rabbit,

six hopping rabbits,

one arty rabbit,

and four cross-country rabbits.

Lion never did find out that the rabbits
had tricked him; who would want to tell him?
After all, the rabbits had just wanted to help.
And from that day on,
Lion was never mean to anyone again.

May I help you carry
your shopping?